Summer Sun Risin'

To Ylla and Aaron, for all your dreams
—W.N-L.

I first thank God. This artwork is dedicated to my Aunt Eleanora E. Tate for

her insight and guidance, and for inspiring me to reach beyond the sun

—D.T.

The artist would like to give special thanks to the Johnson family, Frank, Aretha,
and Shai, who served as models for the characters in this book.

Manufactured in China by Jade Productions

Book design by David Neuhaus/NeuStudio
Book production by The Kids at Our House

The text is set in NeueNeuland.
The illustrations are rendered in oil and acrylic paint on textured Canson paper.

(HC) 10 9 8 7 6 5 4 3
(PB) 20 19 18 17
First Edition

Library of Congress Cataloging-in-Publication Data
Nikola-Lisa, W.
Summer sun risin' / by W. Nikola-Lisa ; illustrated by Don Tate.— 1st ed.
p. cm.
Summary: An African American boy enjoys a summer day on his family's
farm, milking the cows, fishing, and having fun.
ISBN-13: 978-1-58430-034-2 (hc)   ISBN-13: 978-1-58430-252-0 (pb)
[1. Farm life—Fiction. 2. African Americans—Fiction. 3. Stories in rhyme.]
I. Title: Summer sun rising. II. Tate, Don, ill. III. Title.
PZ8.3.N5664 Su 2002   [E]—dc21   2001029720

Summer Sun Risin'

by W. Nikola-Lisa

illustrated by Don Tate

Lee & Low Books Inc.

New York

Wake up, little one—
summer sun's a-risin'!

Rug on the floor,
  light on the wall.
Ma by the bed,
  Pa in the hall.

Dog at the door,
  cat on a chair.
Summer sun's tastin'
  the sweet, sweet air.

Milk in a glass,
egg in a cup.
Toast on a plate
butter side up.

Fritters in a pan,
coffee in the pot.
Summer sun's risin',
makin' it hot.

Birds in the roost,
  kittens in the yarn.
Cows linin' up
  down by the barn.

Pa cracks the door,
  I swing it wide.
Summer sun's shinin',
  floodin' inside.

Chicks in the yard
scratchin' for seed.
Pigs at the trough
waitin' to feed.

Pa by the shed
rollin' out wire.
Summer sun's climbin'
higher and higher.

Hens in the crate,
crates in a row.
Calves all penned,
ready to go.

Truck backin' up,
wheels in the dirt.
Summer sun's glarin',
eyes really hurt.

Train on the tracks,
shiny as a dime.
Ma by the tree
callin' lunchtime.

Pa spreads the cloth,
I set the plates.
Summer sun pauses,
summer sun waits.

Fence on the hill,
   corn in a row.
Hay in the field
   ready to mow.

Pa takes the wheel,
   I work the gears.
Summer sun's blazin',
   burnin' our ears.

Squash on the ground,
   beans on a pole.
Snake chasin' mice
   down a deep hole.

Bees in the hive,
   fruit on the trees.
Summer sun's stirrin'
   a summertime breeze.

Fox in the woods,
hawk in the sky.
Fish in the stream
swimmin' on by.

Pa casts a line,
I check the bait.
Summer sun's slippin'
and the fishin' is great.

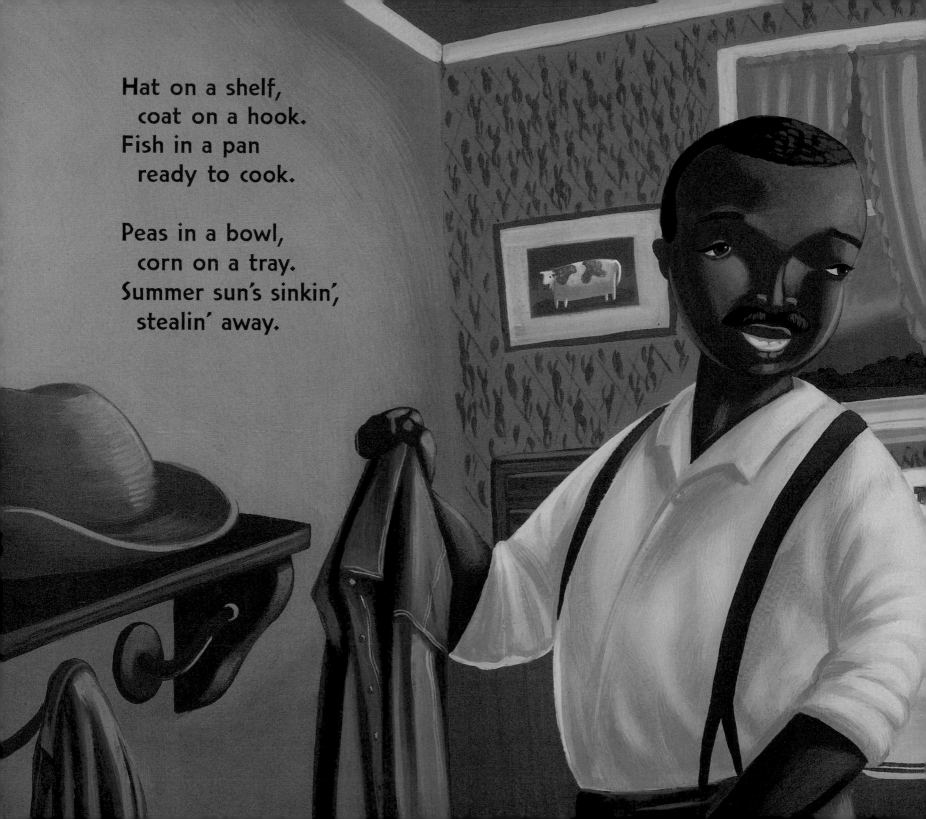

Hat on a shelf,
　coat on a hook.
Fish in a pan
　ready to cook.

Peas in a bowl,
　corn on a tray.
Summer sun's sinkin',
　stealin' away.

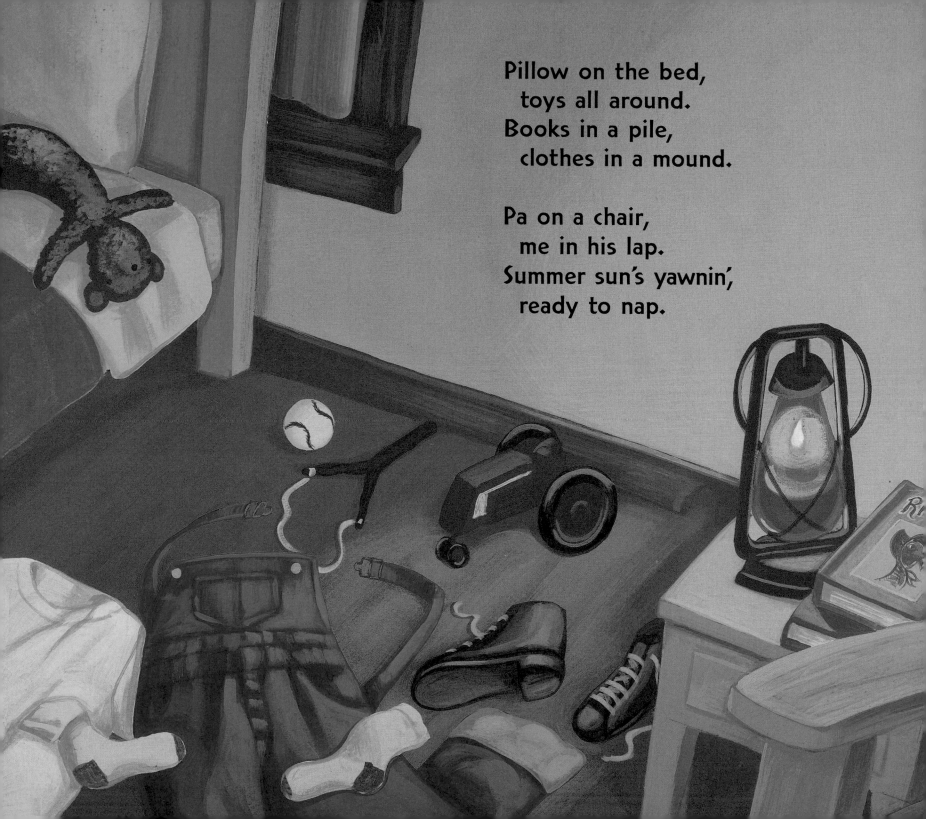

Pillow on the bed,
  toys all around.
Books in a pile,
  clothes in a mound.

Pa on a chair,
  me in his lap.
Summer sun's yawnin',
  ready to nap.

Dog on the stoop,
cat on the rail.
Ma in the swing
readin' the mail.

Pa by the door,
me tucked in bed.
Summer sun's sleepin',
stars overhead.

Summer sun's a-sleepin',
only stars overhead.